- A PART OF THE
SPEAKING UPWORD

MORE than a GIRL

By Tim Lee

This book is dedicated to Brianna, Makayla, Danielle, Layla, Pe'Tehn, Harper Grace, Yahya, Frances, Madeleine, Brooke, Lillian, and Reagan. I trust these words will inspire and empower you and the generations that will follow you. Continue to let your femininity shine. It is a source of your power and the essence of your magic.

Written by Tim Lee
Designed by Christopher Ward

More than a Girl
Copyright ©2021, Tim Lee Creations
ISBN: 978-1-7347640-1-7

I am more than a girl.
I am more than a queen.
I am more than your equal.
I am everything!

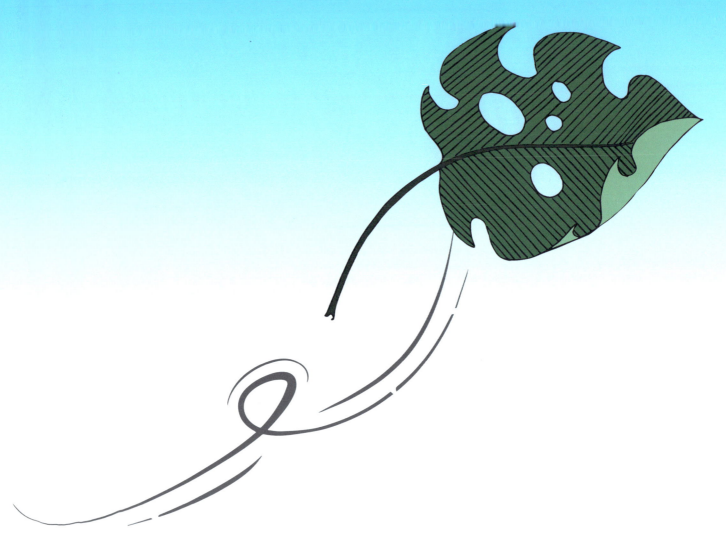

I am the depth of all the oceans.
I am the whisper of the wind.

I am the dancing flames of fire.
I am the soil where life begins.

I am the black sky in the evening.
I am the planet and I am the moon.

I am wisdom and sophistication.
I am courageous and I am strong.

I am magic and I am majesty.
I am the essence of feminine energy.

I don't just run the world,
I am it.
I don't just feed the world,
I heal it.
I won't just change the world,
I'll save it.

Yes, me, a girl...

But I am more than just a girl;

And I am more than just a queen;

And I am more than just your equal;

UpWords

UpWords are positive statements that encourage you to love and believe in yourself.

There are three kinds of UpWords.

1. Flower UpWords
2. Balloon UpWords
3. Butterfly UpWords

Speak UpWords out loud daily!!!

Flowers

Flowers are delicate. They are colorful and fragrant. They bring beauty and variety to a plain landscape. They are gifts to the world. Just like flowers, you are beautiful. You are colorful, and you are a gift to the world. Sometimes, however, you may not feel beautiful. Find a mirror. Look in it. Smile. Say these UpWords.

Flower UpWords are positive statements that help you appreciate and love your physical appearance.

- I am beautiful just the way I am.

- My body is perfectly made.

- I accept myself for who I am today.

- Smiling makes me feel good. I love my smile.

- I love the color of my skin. I love my hair. I love all of me.

- I love my eyes. I love my nose. I love my lips. I love my chin. I love my body. I love my neck. I love my shoulders.

(Say this about as many parts of your body that you can think of).

Balloons

Before balloons are inflated, they are flabby. They dangle. They can stretch. But after they are filled with helium, they expand and can travel to places they couldn't travel before. Your mind is just like a balloon. When you fill it with good information and good habits, it will expand and take your imagination to places you've never been.

Balloon UpWords are positive statements that help you know that you are smart and capable of anything.

- I am intelligent.
- I love to learn new things.
- I am in control of my thoughts.
- My mind is a pearl. I can learn anything in the world!*
- I can do anything I put my mind to.
- If my mind can conceive it and my heart can believe it, I can achieve it!*

*Jesse Lewis Jackson, Sr.

Butterflies

Butterflies are beautiful, magical creatures that represent hope, change, and new life. But they aren't born that way. They are born caterpillars. Caterpillars must go through a process to become a butterfly. And when they complete that process they graduate and get wings. You are like a butterfly. You will go through many things as you grow and mature. Don't give up.

Butterfly UpWords are positive statements that give you wings and help you love your soul.

- I am limitless.
- I can be whatever I want.
- I matter.
- I am confident.
- I am creative.
- I believe in myself.
- I am divine.
- I will succeed.
- I will make a difference.
- I will change the world.
- I embrace change.
- I am love.
- I am powerful.
- I am courageous.
- I am everything.

Words to Know

1. **Womb** – the organ in the lower body of a woman or female mammal where offspring are conceived and in which they gestate before birth; the uterus.

2. **Sophistication** – having a lot of knowledge about the world especially through experience.

3. **Ancestors** – a person from whom one is descended. It usually refers to a remote person, rather than the immediate parents or grandparents.

4. **Majesty** – the quality or state of being impressive and dignified; used as a title for a king, queen, emperor, or empress.

5. **Essence** – the basic part of something.

6. **Femininity** – qualities or attributes regarded as characteristic of women.

7. **Divinity** – the quality or state of being God or a god or goddess.

Made in the USA
Columbia, SC
09 November 2023